The table below shows how important Key Words are.

the first 12 Key Words make up ¼ of those we speak, read and write	the next 20
	68 more words
a further 150	
19,750 words	

The total of these three sections shows that 100 words make up ½ of those we speak, read and write.

⇦ This line represents the first 300 Key Words.

average person's vocabulary

* 12 Key Words make up one quarter of those we read and write.
* 100 Key Words make up half of those we read and write.
* About 300 Key Words account for three quarters of those we read and write.

The Ladybird Key Words Reading Scheme
has three series, each containing
twelve books.

The '**a**' series gradually introduces and
repeats new words.

The parallel '**b**' series provides further
practice of these words, but in a different
context and with different illustrations.

The '**c**' series uses familiar words to teach
phonics in a methodical way, enabling
children to read more difficult words. It also
provides a link with writing.

All three series are written using the same
carefully controlled vocabulary.

A catalogue record for this book is available from the British Library

Published by Ladybird Books Ltd
80 Strand London WC2R 0RL
A Penguin Company
6 8 10 9 7
© LADYBIRD BOOKS LTD MM
LADYBIRD and the device of a Ladybird are trademarks of Ladybird Books Ltd

Key Words
Reading Scheme

6c
Reading with
sounds

written by W. Murray
illustrated by M. Aitchison *and* J.H. Wingfield

1	2	3	4
a	b	c	d

5	6	7	8
e	f	g	h

9	10	11	12
i	l	m	n

13	14	15	16
o	s	t	u

Sounds we know from Books 4c and 5c

p

Here is a pig.
Say the word **pig**.
What is the sound
  when you start to say **pig**?

p

Here is a pen.
Say the word **pen**.
You make the **p** sound
  when you start to say **pen**.

p

Here is a pencil.
Say the word **pencil**.
What is the sound
  when you start to say **pencil**

p

Here is a picture.
Say the word **picture**.
You make the **p** sound
  when you start to say **picture**

p

p

p

p

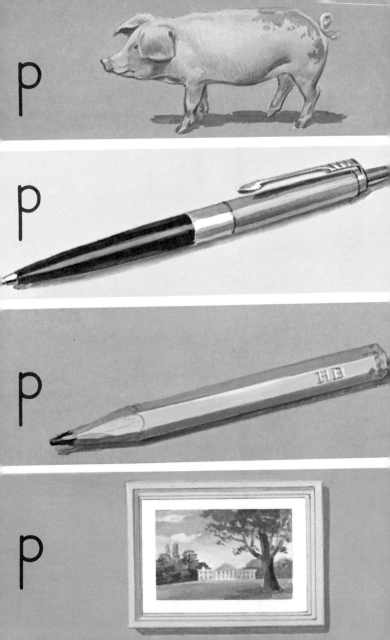

Here is a rabbit.

r

Say the word **rabbit**.

What is the sound
when you start to say **rabbit**

Here is some red.

r

Say the word **red**.

You make the **r** sound
when you start to say **red**.

Here is a road.

r

Say the word **road**.

What is the sound
when you start to say **road**

Here is a room.

r

Say the word **room**.

You make the **r** sound
when you start to say **room**

r

r

r

r

W

Here is some water.

I can say **water**.

It starts with **w**.

W

Here is a woman.

I can say **woman**.

It starts with **w**.

W

Here is a window.

I can say **window**.

It starts with **w**.

W

Here is a wall.

I can say **wall**.

It starts with **w**.

W

W

W

W

j

This is some jam.
You can say **jam**.
It starts with **j**.

j

This is some jelly.
You can say **jelly**.
It starts with **j**.

j

This is a jug.
You can say **jug**.
It starts with **j**.

j

This is a jar.
You can say **jar**.
It starts with **j**.

j

j

j

j

Complete the words as you write
them in your exercise book.
The pictures will help you.

p r w j

1 –ot

2 –ug

3 –et

4 –ar

5 –ag

6 –am

7 –all

8 –eg

The answers are on Page 48.

2

3

4

5

6

7

8

> You can read all the words when
> you make the sounds.

1 It is a jar.
  It is a jar of jam.

2 He has a rag.
  It is a red rag.

3 He is at the top.
  He stops at the top.

4 Look at the cat.
  It is on a rug.

5 She gets a pot.
  She puts jam in the pot.

6 The dog is wet.
  He rubs the dog.

7 She gets the ham.
  She puts ham in the pan.

8 She has pegs.
  She has lots of pegs.

k

We see a key.

We can say **key**.

It starts with **k**.

---

k

We see a kettle.

We can say **kettle**.

It starts with **k**.

---

k

We see a king.

We can say **king**.

It starts with **k**.

---

k

We see a kitten.

We can say **kitten**.

It starts with **k**.

k

k

k

k

Look at the van.

V

You say **van**.

It starts with **v**.

Look at the vase.

V

You say **vase**.

It starts with **v**.

Look at the vine.

V

You say **vine**.

It starts with **v**.

Look at the violin.

V

You say **violin**.

It starts with **v**.

x as in **box**

X

x as in **fox**

y

y for **yellow**

Z

z for **zebra**

and

z for **zoo**

x

y

z

Complete the words as you write
them in your exercise book.
The pictures will help you.

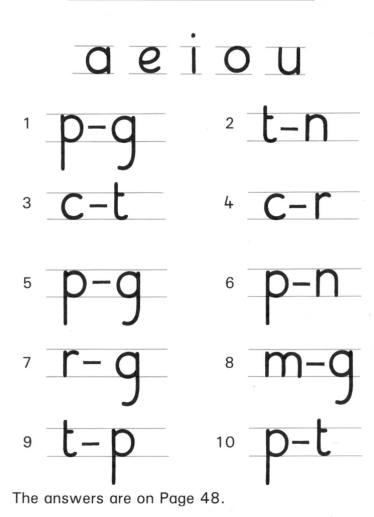

a e i o u

1 p-g

2 t-n

3 c-t

4 c-r

5 p-g

6 p-n

7 r-g

8 m-g

9 t-p

10 p-t

The answers are on Page 48.

qu for **quarter**

Here is a quarter.

qu for **queen**

Here is a queen.

qu for **quill**

Here is a quill.

qu

qu

qu

Grandfather and Grandmother write to say that they want to go away to the sea. They want Dad and the children to look after their dog, their house and their garden when they are away.

Mum reads the letter to Peter and Jane.

Jane says, "Good. I want to look after the house."

Peter says, "Yes, it will be fun. I will take the dog out every day, and we can all look after the garden."

"Let's write a letter to Grandmother and Grandfather," says Jane.

"Yes," says Peter, "we will do it now."

Copy out and complete –

1 Mum reads to —eter and Jane.

2 Grandfather and Grandmother —ant to go away.

3 Peter and —ane will help.

4 Peter says, "—es, I want to do it."

The answers are on Page 48.

The children write to their grandmother and grandfather.

Jane has a pencil and she writes down the words. Mum and Peter help her. They tell Jane what to write. Jane writes —

Dear Grandmother and Grandfather,

Thank you for your letter. We will look after your house and garden when you are at the sea. We like to help you very much.

We will take the dog out every day for a walk and we will look after the birds and flowers.

Have a good time at the sea.

Love, from

Jane and Peter.

Copy out and complete —

1   They —ant —o write.

2   Jane —as a —encil.

3   They like to help —ery much.

4   We w—ll take the d—g out.

The answers are on Page 49.

Peter's father takes his own father and mother to the station by car. Peter and Jane are with them. The children are going to see their grandmother and grandfather off.

At the station Peter and his sister help Grandmother and Grandfather out of the car. Dad has the bags.

They find the train in the station. Soon Grandfather and Grandmother are in the train.

"Look after each other," says Dad.

"Yes, we will," says Grandfather.

"Have a good time," say the children.

Then the train pulls out of the station.

Copy out and complete –

1 Peter's —ather has a car.

2 Dad has the —ags.

3 Peter and Jane look —p at the train.

4 The children are —ot in the train.

The answers are on Page 49.

Here are Dad, Peter and Jane at Grandfather's house. They have come by car. Jane has her doll, Ann, with her today.

They go into the house. They have been here lots of times before. The children like to come to this house. They love their grandfather and grandmother very much.

Soon they start to work. Jane does the work in the house and Peter and his father go into the garden.

Peter looks for Grandfather's dog. He wants to take him for a walk.

Copy out and complete –

1   They are —t their grandfather's house.

2   They —o into the house.

3   —oon they start to work.

4   Peter —ooks for the —og.

The answers are on Page 49.

Peter is out with the dog. He takes him where he can run about.

It is a very hot day. Peter finds it best to walk under the trees because it is not so hot there. The trees are by the water.

Peter sits on a wall by the water. He looks at some other boys as they play with a ball. One of the boys lets the ball go into the water.

Peter tells the dog to go into the water. The dog jumps in and gets the ball for the boys.

Copy out and complete –

1 The —og likes to —un.
2 The boy l—ts the ball go —nto the water.
3 The dog —an get the —all.
4 He —umps in —or the ball.

The answers are on Page 50.

Peter and his father are in Grandfather's garden. Pat is with them.

Jane is with an old friend of her grandmother who lives next door. This friend is going to let her have some eggs.

Peter's father has work to do. Peter helps him and then he has a game with the dog. The dog likes to jump for a ball and to run after it. It is not so hot now.

There is some water in the garden. Soon Peter lets the ball go into the water. ''I'll get it,'' he says.

Copy out and complete –

1   Jane has one, two, three, four, five, si— eggs.
2   The dog —uns and —umps.
3   It is —ot so —ot now.
4   ''Loo—,'' says Peter, ''the ball is in the water.''

The answers are on Page 50.

Jane comes out of the house into the garden. She sees that the ball is in the water and that Peter is going to get it.

"Don't get wet, Peter," she says.

But Peter is soon in the water.

"Help," he says. "Help me, Dad. Help me, Jane. I am in the water. Help me to get out."

Then the dog jumps into the water. He wants to play with Peter.

Dad and Jane run to pull Peter out of the water.

They get him out, but he is very wet.

Copy out and complete —

1 Dad works in the —arden.
2 "Help —e, Jane," says Peter.
3 The dog —ees Peter in the water.
4 Peter is —ery w—t.

The answers are on Page 50.

Jane is in the garden. She can see some birds as they fly round the trees. She knows that her grandmother and grandfather love birds.

"Grandmother gives them something to eat every day," Jane says. "They look as if they want to eat now. I must get something for them."

She gets some cake and puts it out for the birds. Soon they come down to eat it.

Jane looks at the birds as they eat the cake. Then she gets some flowers from the garden for the friend who lives next door.

Copy out and complete –

1   Jane is —n the garden.
2   She looks at the birds —s they fly round the trees.
3   Jane —ets some cake for the birds.
4   The birds eat the —ake.

The answers are on Page 51.

Grandmother and Grandfather have come home today. They have had a good time by the sea.

Here is Grandmother with Jane. She takes off her hat as she sits down to have some tea and talk to Jane.

Jane tells her about the house, the garden, the dog and the birds. She says that Grandmother's friend next door gave them some eggs.

Then Jane talks about her own friends. She tells Grandmother about Mr and Mrs Green, Bob, Mary and Molly, about Pam, and about old Tom who lives by the sea.

Copy out and complete –

1 Grandmother takes off her h—t.
2 They have —ad a good time.
3 Jane talks about Pa— and B—b.
4 Jane talks about old T—m.

The answers are on Page 51.

Grandfather thanks the children for the help they gave when he was away. He says he will take them to the Zoo.

Off they go the next day. Grandfather has no car, so they go by train.

At the Zoo they walk round for some time and then they have something to eat. Then Peter says, "I want to go on the elephant."

Here he is on the elephant. Jane looks at an ostrich. "What a big bird," she says.

The children have a good time at the Zoo, and then they go home. They thank Grandfather very much.

Copy out and complete –

1 Peter and Jane go to the —oo.
2 The children —ike the —oo.
3 Peter gets —p on the —lephant.
4 They thank Grandfather —ery —uch.

The answers are on Page 51.

Pages 48 to 51 give the answers to the
written exercises in this book.

Page 14	1	pot	2	rug
	3	wet	4	jar
	5	rag	6	jam
	7	wall	8	peg

Page 24	1	pig	2	tin
	3	cat	4	car
	5	peg	6	pen
	7	rug	8	mug
	9	top	10	pot

Page 28   1   Mum reads to Peter and Jane.

2   Grandfather and Grandmother
want to go away.

3   Peter and Jane will help.

4   Peter says, "Yes, I want to do it."

Page 30   1   They want to write.

2   Jane has a pencil.

3   They like to help very much.

4   We will take the dog out.

Page 32   1   Peter's father has a car.

2   Dad has the bags.

3   Peter and Jane look up at the train.

4   The children are not in the train.

Page 34   1   They are at their grandfather's house.

2   They go into the house.

3   Soon they start to work.

4   Peter looks for the dog.

Page 36 1 The dog likes to run.

  2 The boy lets the ball go into the water.

  3 The dog can get the ball.

  4 He jumps in for the ball.

Page 38 1 Jane has one, two, three, four, five, six eggs.

  2 The dog runs and jumps.

  3 It is not so hot now.

  4 "Look," says Peter, "the ball is in the water."

Page 40 1 Dad works in the garden.

  2 "Help me, Jane," says Peter.

  3 The dog sees Peter in the water.

  4 Peter is very wet.

Page 42 1 Jane is in the garden.

2 She looks at the birds as they fly round the trees.

3 Jane gets some cake for the birds.

4 The birds eat the cake.

Page 44 1 Grandmother takes off her hat.

2 They have had a good time.

3 Jane talks about Pam and Bob.

4 Jane talks about old Tom.

Page 46 1 Peter and Jane go to the Zoo.

2 The children like the Zoo.

3 Peter gets up on the elephant.

4 They thank Grandfather very much.

Now read Book 7a

Learning by sounds

If children learn the sounds of letters and how to blend them with the other letter sounds (eg. c-a-t) they can tackle new words independently (eg. P-a-t).

In the initial stages it is best if these phonic words are already known to the learner.

However, not all English words can be learned in this way as the English language is not purely phonetic (eg. t-h-e).

In general a 'mixed' approach to reading is recommended. Some words are learned by blending the sounds of their letters and others by look-and-say, whole word or sentence methods.

This book provides the link with writing for the words in Readers 6a and 6b.